S0-DOO-818

Afro Unicorn®

# A Magical Day

April Showers
Illustrated by Anthony Conley

A Random House PICTUREBACK® Book

Random House 🏠 New York

Text and art copyright © 2023 by Afro Unicorn, Inc.
All rights reserved. Published in the United States by Random House Children's Books, a division
of Penguin Random House LLC, New York.
Pictureback, Random House, and the Random House colophon are registered trademarks
of Penguin Random House LLC.
Visit us on the Web!
rhcbooks.com
Library of Congress Cataloging-in-Publication Data is available upon request.
ISBN 978-0-593-70285-7 (trade) — ISBN 978-0-593-70286-4 (ebook)
Printed in the United States of America
10 9 8 7 6 5 4 3 2
Random House Children's Books supports the First Amendment and celebrates the right to read.

You're invited to
Magical's birthday party!

Everyone in the enchanted land of Afronia was invited to Magical's birthday!

Her best friends, Unique and Divine, couldn't wait for the party that afternoon. Their Kindness Crowns glowed with excitement!

Unique sang in her super-voice:

> **"It's going to be a Magical day!**
> **We'll make it special in every way."**

"We need to surprise Magical with a special present!" exclaimed Divine.

But how do you surprise a friend who has superpowers?

All unicorns had superpowers, and their Kindness Crowns made them even stronger.

Divine used her super-strength to help others.

Unique's super-songs inspired and encouraged everyone.

And Magical was the most powerful of all: she had the power to read what was in your heart.

Magical rushed into the garden. "My dear friends, there is no time for celebrations!" She had lost her Kindness Crown, and her superpowers wouldn't work well without it.

"Have you seen my crown?" Magical asked.
Divine shook her head.

The two friends started their search in the forest of the Afro Saurus.

"Where's that missing crown?" Divine wondered aloud. "We must find it before the party!"

Unique trailed behind. "I have a secret I need to share. Let's go to Star Cove—we'll find the crown there."

Unique had taken Magical's crown to Star Cove to sprinkle stardust on it—and had forgotten it there. "I wanted the crown to sparkle just right so Magical's birthday would be extra bright."

Their friend Hummi was waiting for them at Star Cove.
"There you are, Unique!" exclaimed Hummi. "I was
guarding the crown, like you asked. But . . ."

The crown had slipped between two shimmering star-shaped rocks.

"Oh no! Oh no! Don't let it be so!" Unique cried.

There was not much time left! It was up to Divine and her super-strength to save the day.

But Divine's powers were not enough.
"You can do it if you work *together*!" cheered Hummi.
"Sing a super-song, Unique."

Unique began to sing encouragingly:
"I believe in our friendship. I believe in you.
If you believe in *yourself*, there's nothing you can't do!"

Inspired by Unique's beautiful song, Divine tried
again and *believed* it could happen.

It worked! The crown came loose!

"Believing is the greatest superpower of all!" Hummi said.

Back at the castle, Unique and Divine found Magical.
"I'm sorry, Magical. Please don't frown," sang Unique.
"I wanted to surprise you, so I took your crown."
Magical was so happy to see her crown again.

"I should have asked. I know that now. I hope you'll forgive me somehow," said Unique.

"You are always honest and kind, Unique, and that's what counts," Magical said.

It was finally party time!
"But we never got Magical a special present," Unique fretted.

"The friendship in your hearts is the brightest present of all," Magical assured them.

Unique was filled with joy. She sang:
"Have a Magical day!
You're unique. You're divine.
We all have a crown
that glows when we're kind!"

All was right in Afronia again.
"Hooray for Magic!
From our hearts we say,
have a hap-hap-happy,
Magical birthday!"